Perfect Revenge

K.L. Denman

ORCA BOOK PUBLISHERS

Orca currents

Library and Archives Canada Cataloguing in Publication

Denman, K.L., 1957-
Perfect revenge / written by K.L. Denman.

(Orca currents)
ISBN 978-1-55469-103-6 (bound).--ISBN 978-1-55469-102-9 (pbk.)

I. Title. II. Series.

PS8607.E64P47 2009   jC813'.6   C2008-907664-8

Summary: Stripped of her popularity, Lizzie is willing to do anything to
exact her revenge. She's even willing to turn to magic.

First published in the United States, 2009
Library of Congress Control Number: 2008942005

Orca Book Publishers gratefully acknowledges the support for its publishing
programs provided by the following agencies: the Government of Canada
through the Book Publishing Industry Development Program and the
Canada Council for the Arts, and the Province of British Columbia
through the BC Arts Council and the Book Publishing Tax Credit.

Cover design by Teresa Bubela
Cover photography by Getty Images

Orca Book Publishers
PO Box 5626, Station B
Victoria, BC Canada
V8R 6S4

Orca Book Publishers
PO Box 468
Custer, WA USA
98240-0468

www.orcabook.com
Printed and bound in Canada.
Printed on 100% PCW recycled paper.

12 11 10 09 • 4 3 2 1

For Mom, who exemplifies the beauty of
empathy and the joy found in laughter.

I invoke the power of three,
But stand aside to relate,
There's a duo found in trinity,
Kindred spirits who create.
She of the high meadows,
And the goddess of the moon,
They peer among the shadows
For word-spells out of tune.
I thank this special pair
Without naming, not this time,
For while they're not so holy,
They would spare you this rhyme.

*The universe is full of magical things, patiently
waiting for our wits to grow sharper.*
—Eden Phillpotts

chapter one

Everything is going my way. It's no accident that this is how it is. I've earned it. Like this morning, I put on my new skirt and my new lip gloss, and the mirror says it's all perfect. Combine that with my amazing shiny hair, and I'm good to go.

It's too bad I'm only going to school, but that's okay. If nothing else, school is great for hanging with my group of friends. Not just any group, *the* group in my grade. They're gathered in the usual place, the covered area by the side door. When I get there, everyone's all, "Hey, Lizzie! How's it going, Lizzie? Oooh! That skirt is hot! Where'd you get it? You always find the best stuff!"

And then, a whisper, "There he is! Omigod, Liz, it's him."

It *is* him. Kyle, my crush.

"Lizzie, don't look now, but he's walking this way!"

I don't look. I say something to Haley about her hair. I pretend that Kyle doesn't exist right until the last minute when I can *feel* him passing. And then I look. It's no more than a quick glance in his direction, totally casual. Our eyes connect. I smile.

He smiles back!

And that's it. He goes by and I laugh with my friends like it was nothing. Of course, they saw the smile. Haley says, "He likes you, Liz. I can tell. He is *so* over Rachel."

Rachel, the pathetic wannabe.

It's like this. I am in the group of girls who have "it." We naturally shine. If the girls in our grade were an eye-shadow palette, my group would be the main color base, the glowing center. The other groups would be the smaller pockets of color, optional extras. Sometimes their colors blend with ours. Rachel's copycat group is like a beige highlight, useful sometimes— but not necessary. Rachel so wishes she could be part of *us*, like she once was.

She still gets to talk to us sometimes. She still has access to certain information, like if one of us wants something, she hears about it. So she *knew* about my interest in Kyle, and she had the nerve to move in on him anyway. It was just, like, so wrong of her to do that. This is why I had to do what I did.

I turn to Haley. "They lasted for, what, five days?"

She giggles. "If that. Once he heard about you know what, he was done with her."

I shrug and say, "Did I mention how nice it is that your Josh is best friends with my Kyle?"

She nods. "You did mention it. But he's not *your* Kyle yet, girl."

I blink at her. "You know it's going to happen. You saw his smile. He wants me. And you know he's in my science class, right?"

She does an eye roll. "I think you might have told me, like, fifty times."

"That is so not the point. It's just that I think it would be perfect to get him for a lab partner. Any ideas on how I can make that happen?"

Her brow wrinkles in thought, but then she sighs. "Sorry. The only thing I've got is, you ask the teacher for a switch. But then he could stick you with anyone, right? Although..."

"What?" I ask.

Haley arches her brows. "How are your grades in science?"

It's my turn to do an eye roll.

"Then how about this. You tell the teacher you need a better partner, someone who's good at the labs. Kyle is really smart."

"He is?" I ask.

"Oh yeah, for sure. Didn't you know that?" Haley blinks a few times, waiting for me to show gratitude for this information. When I merely shrug, she adds, "Josh told me that Kyle gets, like, ninety-five percent on *everything*. He studies really hard."

"Are you kidding?" I need a moment to consider this. Kyle is cute *and* he's smart? Do I want a boyfriend who's smarter than me? Hmmm. On the other hand...I grin at Haley and say, "It's worth a try, right?"

Science isn't until last period. The day drags past—an off day with no more Kyle sightings. When the wait is finally over, I get to class a bit early. As I'm walking in, Rachel is walking out. She says, "Oh. Hey, Lizzie. How's it going?"

I give her my widest smile and say, "Great. How's it going with you?"

She smiles back. "It's all good. I'm glad we ran into each other. I have something for you." She pulls a folded wad of paper from her purse and holds it out.

"What's this?" I ask.

"Take it," she urges. "It's a gift. Just to show there's no hard feelings."

I raise my eyebrows. "Hard feelings? Why would there be hard feelings?"

She shrugs. "No reason. Anyway, I just want to give you this. Here."

I have no choice but to take the paper. "Thanks," I say, as I stuff it into my purse.

"You're welcome," she says. There's something in her eyes that doesn't match her smile, and I get a little chill.

chapter two

The chill from Rachel melts when I spot Kyle on the other side of the lab. He's early too. I take my seat and gaze in the general direction of the teacher. Mr. Sparks happens to be standing near Kyle, and when I slide my glance a little to the left, omigod! Our eyes meet. Not mine and Mr. Sparks' eyes, mine and Kyle's.

Kyle grins and stands up. He's coming my way when Mr. Sparks says, "Be seated, everyone. Books on the floor. Pens and calculators only for this exam."

Exam?

Someone asks, "Are we allowed scrap paper?"

Mr. Sparks says, "Yes, scrap paper is allowed. But be careful. I'll be checking that the scrap is blank."

Exam?

I turn to my current lab partner, Mandy. She's okay, totally dope for someone in the optional shadow colors. The way our school just randomly sticks us in classes, backup people like her are necessary for social survival. I ask her, "Did you know we're having an exam today?"

"Wow," she says, "can you believe it?"

"Did the teacher even tell us?" I ask.

She shrugs. "I don't know. Should I ask him?"

I blink at her. "Sure."

Mandy puts up her hand. When Mr. Sparks notices, he says, "Yes?"

"Um, Mr. Sparks. Did you, like, warn us about this?"

He sighs. "Yes, Mandy. I mentioned it

several times. And it's been posted on the blackboard for a week."

"Oh. Okay."

Mr. Sparks sweeps his gaze around the room, sees that most everyone is settled and starts handing out the exam. I sneak a peek at Kyle, and he looks totally serious, like he's already focused on his test.

I have no idea what this exam is about. Periodic table of the elements? Forms of energy? What have we been doing in here anyway? I know what I've been doing, and it wasn't science. Unless a crush is part of biology? The thought makes me giggle, but I cover that up with a cough and scrounge in my purse for a pen. Oh, and some scrap paper too. That's allowed.

My hand closes around the wad of paper Rachel gave me. I pull that out along with a pen. Mr. Sparks drops the test on our table and moves on. When everyone has a copy, he says, "All right, class. You'll have the entire period to write the exam. If you finish before the bell, please remain seated and use that time to review your answers.

This counts for twenty percent of your final grade. You may begin."

A tense silence descends on the room— the silence that only happens during exams. The only sounds are those of paper shuffling, throats clearing and the scratching of pens. I look at the first question.

1. Gastric juice is composed of mucus, hydrochloric acid, water and digestive enzymes. The purpose of the mucus is to:

A. digest proteins into smaller particles

B. prevent the gastric juice from digesting the stomach

C. assist the hydrochloric acid with digestion

D. prevent heartburn from occurring

I feel sick. Mucus? I didn't pay attention when Mr. Sparks talked about that stuff. I couldn't. I mean, who wants to know about mucus? Not me. Isn't science supposed to be about satisfying curiosity? Who was the geek that was curious about mucus?

I glance at my wad of paper and realize that *this* makes me curious. What does Rachel's note say? Judging by the size of it, she had a lot to say.

I unfold the wad and...what the heck? It looks like the science test. She gave me her test? Where's the note? I start flipping through the pages, looking on both sides, and I can't find her note anywhere. And then Mr. Sparks is behind me, peering over my shoulder.

"Well, well," he says. "Lizzie Lane. This is a surprise."

"Excuse me?" I say.

"Absolutely," he says. His voice gets louder. "You are excused. You may go directly to the principal's office and wait for me there."

"Uh...why?"

He snorts. Literally snorts. "The consequences of cheating aren't obvious?"

"Cheating?"

"Oh, for pity's sake! I find you with my exam answer key and you're going to pretend it's invisible? Or am I supposed to believe it just magically appeared on your table?"

"Answer key?" He's getting through to me now. "You mean this exam has the answers on it?" I look again, and sure enough, the answers are typed right beside the questions. I wasn't looking for type print, I was looking for handwriting. Rachel's handwriting.

Rachel.

She did this.

"Elizabeth. The principal's office. Now!"

"I can explain."

Mr. Sparks shakes his head. "I'm sure you can. And you'll have your chance in the office. Are you going?"

I have no choice. My hands tremble as I gather my purse and books. My face burns. My legs feel wobbly. I cast a look around the room, and all eyes are on me. All, that is, except Kyle's. The way he is so harshly *not* looking at me makes me feel he'd rather look at mucus.

chapter three

It's easy to give people the wrong impression.
Sometimes, I even give myself the wrong
impression. Like thinking life was good
and that I was in control of it.

I have to wait outside the principal's
office until after the final bell. When Mr.
Sparks finally shows up, and I tell them
what happened, they don't believe me.

Mr. Sparks says, "Rachel is a model
student, while you, Lizzie, quite frankly,
are not."

"Science isn't exactly my thing," I say.

Mr. Sparks ignores this and keeps talking. "Also, you're often late to class and today I noticed that you were early."

The principal says, "We will be contacting your parents."

Mr. Sparks says, "Your grade on the exam is zero."

Not to be outdone, the principal leans forward and says, "And our usual policy for cheating is suspension from school."

I feel like I'm going to cry.

"However," he adds, "since this is your first offence, we will consider one week of detention. This will depend upon you."

"Me?" I squeak.

"That's correct. If you return tomorrow with a written apology for Mr. Sparks, you may be allowed to serve a week of detention."

Such a deal, I think. I desperately want to get out of there and run to the comfort of my circle of friends, so I simply nod. They release me.

The empty hallways feel creepy, and

I don't even bother to go to my locker. I head straight for the covered area, but when I get there, nobody's there! Not even Haley. I pull out my cell phone to call her, but the battery is dead. It gets worse. I have to walk home by myself. It feels so strange and lonely. I keep my eyes down. I don't want anyone to recognize me, Lizzie Lane, walking alone.

When I finally get home, the house is empty too. Mom and Dad are still at work, which is normal, but it's not too often that I go home alone. I usually bring friends with me or I go to their place. It's like I've entered some weird alternate universe.

I grab the phone and head out into the backyard to call Haley. She finally answers on the fourth ring and her voice sounds cold. "Oh. Hey, Lizzie."

That's it? No stream of questions about what happened to me? I say, "Omigod, Haley! You won't believe it."

There's a tiny space of silence, and then she says, "Actually, I heard."

"You did? So you know about Rachel?"

"Rachel?" Haley still sounds cold. "What does she have to do with anything?"

"Everything!" I yell. "She made it look like I was cheating on a science exam."

"Oh, come on, Lizzie. You don't expect me to believe that, do you?"

I say, "Huh?"

"Look, everyone knows what happened. I mean, enough people saw it, right? And I can figure things out too, you know. Like, I tell you that Kyle's really smart so you have to try and be smart too? Just so you know, he hates you now."

I can't believe this is happening. It must be some sort of nightmare. I give my hair a tug to see if I can feel it. I don't know why that's supposed to change nightmares, but I've heard of people doing stuff like that.

"So yeah," Haley says, "I've gotta go. We're all going to the mall."

"But," I splutter, "you don't even know what happened! Rachel gave me that answer key. She said it was a gift. I thought it was a note."

"That's pathetic, girl. She isn't even in your class. You know, you've been really mean to Rachel. She's not a complete loser. And you telling everyone about her lopsided boobs to get her away from Kyle—was that even true?"

"I told you, she showed me! In grade six. She has to stuff one side of her bra to even out. And I'm not the one who wrote it on the bathroom walls or told Josh! You—"

She cuts me off. "Yeah, I so believed you. It's not like she could prove it wrong, is it? Not unless she wants to go around flashing everyone. And now you're trying to pin your cheating on her too? Get real!" And Haley hangs up.

I stare at the phone. I throw the phone. If Rachel was here right now, I'd throw her too. Or something. My head feels like it's on fire, my stomach too. In fact, my entire body is burning. Bit by bit, the extent of damage caused by Rachel's little gift starts to sink in. I'm in trouble at school. My parents are going to be furious. My friends have ditched me. My crush hates me.

I've never felt so much anger. Rachel is going to pay for this! And then I collapse on the lawn and start sobbing, just wailing like I've never wailed before.

I do that for a while, long enough to feel like a blob of melted jelly. I start hiccupping, and that makes me cry more. There's nothing left of me but hopeless pain and rage. And then I hear a voice. It occurs to me that I've been hearing it for a while.

It says, "Hey. Are you hurt? You need help?"

I lift my head and look around. There's the back door, the patio, the fence. I hear it again.

"It's Lizzie, right? Are you okay?"

There's a tree by the fence, and the voice is coming from there. From the tree. That's it, for sure I've lost my mind now too. I moan and lie back on the grass.

"I'm coming over, okay?"

I sit up again and stare at the tree. It's coming over? Part of me knows I better get out of there, fast, but my body refuses to move. My brain is saying, "go," but my body's just not getting it.

Sure enough, the tree starts rustling, and I think I'm going to faint now, just check out, when a long skinny leg emerges from the leaves. That leg is followed by another. Both legs are clad in striped socks. Seriously, red-and-black-striped socks.

The legs dangle for a moment and then an entire body drops to the ground. There is nothing else for me to do but scream. I close my eyes, throw back my head and howl.

chapter four

"Hey! Whoa! Wow, you're really messed up, huh?"

The voice sounds human. It even sounds friendly. I crack open an eye, and there's a girl standing over me.

"Should I call an ambulance?" she asks.

"An ambulance?" I croak.

"Yeah. You don't look like you're bleeding or broken or anything, but your face is all red and swollen. Do you have allergies? Did you eat something bad?"

Her face is puckered with concern, but I recognize her.

I mutter, "You're that new kid from next door."

"Yup. I'm Stella." She tilts her head to one side and smiles. The sunlight flashes off her braces and practically blinds me. She adds, "You're Lizzie, right?"

"Yeah."

"So, what's wrong?" she asks.

I sit up and squint at her. "Have you been spying on me?"

"Uh, no. But I heard you crying and I climbed the tree by the fence to see what was wrong. You're not physically injured though, are you?"

I heave a sigh and say, "You wouldn't understand."

She plops down on the lawn and says, "Try me."

I look at her and think this is incredibly weird because *she's* incredibly weird. She's not the sort of person I'd normally ever talk to. I've seen her around a few times since she moved in next door, but one look at her was all I needed to know she wasn't my type. I mean, the kid dresses like a Raggedy Ann doll. She's so thin she looks like a collection of twigs. And her hair! It's this wild mass of black curls that frizz around her head like an alien life-form.

But I start talking. I tell her everything that happened to me, and she listens. Really listens. When I'm done talking, I feel better but also a little worried. Is talking to someone like her yet another sign that life as I've known it is over?

"Sounds like that Rachel girl is really mean," Stella says. "Why would she do something like that to you?"

"I don't know," I sniff. "But I'll tell you this. She's going to pay. I don't know how yet, but I'll get her back."

Stella grins. I blink to avoid the flash off the metal, but it doesn't happen this time. She looks at me sideways and says, "I know what you need."

"You do?" I ask.

"Oh yeah." She nods. In that gesture I find some hope. Her nod is so certain.

"So tell me," I say.

"You need to work a little magick," she says.

I stare at her. "Magick? You're making fun of me?"

"No. I wouldn't do that." She shakes her head. "I'm totally serious. I know some magick. My baba has been teaching me."

I roll my eyes. "Your baba? What's that?"

"My grandmother," Stella says. "She's from the old country and she knows plenty."

"You are serious, aren't you?" I ask. "I mean, you actually believe in this stuff?"

"For sure I believe it. I've seen it work." Stella frowns and bends her head to pluck at the grass. "Although, I'm not really supposed to tell just anyone about it."

"Why not?"

"Because," she says, "it's sort of a family secret. Well, maybe not just for blood family, but for those who have respect. It's not a game."

Of all the things Stella might have said, this bit about secrets and respect sounds convincing. "So you're saying that if I learn how to do this, I could get back at Rachel?"

Stella nods her head vigorously. "I know the perfect revenge spell."

Perfect revenge. The words waft into my steamed brain like a cool breeze. Ahh. The dreary darkness of misery parts to make way for hope. I start to imagine things. A wart on Rachel's nose—a giant fuzzy wart. And tufts of hair growing out of her ears. Oh, and what about armpits that pour smelly sweat? I'm just warming up when Stella cuts in.

"You'll have to learn a few basics first. The revenge spell is tricky."

"Tricky?" I ask. "What do you mean?"

"I mean," she says, "whatever you send out magickally, will come back on you threefold."

"Say what?" I ask.

"It's like this." Stella hesitates, then begins to twirl a tuft of hair in her finger. No wonder it looks like an alien life-form. The twirling is intense. "When you work magick you're working with the power of nature. It's like shaping or bending the energy to your will. But before you draw power from the source, you need to align with it. Does this sound complicated?"

"Uh, yeah."

"Darn," she says. "There's a lot to explain. It's hard to know where to start."

I'm getting suspicious. I think Stella is just making this up. I mean, how hard can it be if *she* does it? "Why don't you give me an example? Or better yet, a demonstration."

She laughs. "You want to see me vanish or something?"

"No." Although now that she's mentioned it..."I just want you to keep it simple. Isn't there some kindergarten magick you can show me?"

"Hmmm," she says. "All right. How about this. I'll teach you an easy spell, and when you're ready, you can try it yourself."

"Sounds good."

"Okay, here goes." Stella sits up straight and says, "Repeat after me. On the count of one, the spell's begun."

"On the count of one, the spell's begun."
I get a teensy little tingle in my spine.

"On the count of two, let the magick ring true."

I repeat that, and the hair on my arms stands up.

"On the count of three, the magick is me."

As I repeat the last line, I feel a definite vibe. "Wow. Now what?"

"Well," Stella says, "that's a simple incantation. What you do is think of something you want to have happen. You get the idea firmly in your head. Maybe you light a candle. Then you say the words and picture the thing you want to happen."

"That's it?" I ask. "And then it happens?"

"Maybe not right away," she says. "Magick works in its own time. You have to be patient."

I'm about to tell her that sucks when I hear my mom's car pull up to the house. "Oh no," I moan.

"What?" Stella asks.

"I think the principal was going to call my mom at work. I'm in for it now."

Stella shakes her head. "Won't your mother believe you when you explain?"

"I don't know." I shrug. "Guess I'll find out."

"I better go," Stella says. "But there are some important things about the magick I haven't finished explaining. Maybe I'll talk to you later?"

"Yeah," I say. "Later."

chapter five

To complete the Worst Day of My Life, I get the Worst Evening of My Life. My parents don't believe that Rachel would play such a dirty trick on me. They know Rachel's parents. Mom says, "They're lovely people. Simply lovely. And Rachel is always so polite. I don't know why you two can't be friends."

Dad says, "I'm very disappointed in you, Elizabeth."

I say, "My life is over. I wish I were dead."

That gets them to back off a little. Mom pats my shoulder and says, "There, there. You don't mean that. You know, there's probably a simple explanation. Maybe Rachel picked up the test key by mistake. Then she got it mixed up with her note to you."

This is far-fetched and we all know it, but we decide that must have been what happened. Everything was one big accident. We also decide the principal and Mr. Sparks are unlikely to believe this.

Dad says, "You're going to have to write that note of apology, Lizzie."

"I don't want a week of detention." I fold my arms across my chest. "No way. I'd rather be suspended. I don't want to go back to that school, ever!"

Dad folds *his* arms across his chest. "Young lady, you are going to write that note and you are going to attend school. You may even consider doing extra science work while in detention. You need to make up the lost marks."

"But I didn't do anything! This is so NOT fair!"

"Where did you get the idea that life is fair?" he asks.

"I don't know." I glare at him. "Maybe from you?"

"Well," he says, "I must apologize for that. Life isn't fair. Never has been, never will be. End of story. Go write the note."

He has that look on his face that says the discussion is over. He hardly ever has that look, but when he does, he means it.

This is the note I write:

Dear Mr. Sparks,
I apologize for having your exam key in my hands. I promise that what happened in class today will never happen to me again. I intend to make sure of that.
Sincerely,
Lizzie Lane

I show the note to Mom and she sighs. "I suppose it will have to do."

The next thing I do is call Haley. She won't even come to the phone. Her little brother says, "Haley's busy right now. She's, uh, taking a crap."

I hear Haley shrieking in the background as he hangs up, and I know she told him to say that. Not the part about the crap, just that she was busy. I quite like her little brother sometimes.

The only thing left for me to do is plot my revenge against Rachel. I think about the magick, and it all seems lame. What was I doing talking to Stella? Worse yet, I was slightly sucked in by her. I must have been so overcome with the tragic state of my life that I wasn't in my right mind. The only problem is that I can't get that spell out of my head. It keeps repeating in there, and it starts to creep me out. Maybe it does have some power.

There's only one way to find out. I'll do an experiment. That's scientific, isn't it? I'm making up lost marks already. I wish. All right, what was it Stella said? She said I need to focus. And light a candle. And picture something I want. I think that was it. So I light a candle and try to figure out what I want.

I think about hosting my own fashion TV talk show, but that's sort of off base. Sure, I want that, but it'll have to wait. Right now, I want something bad to happen to Rachel. Like, for starters, she wakes up tomorrow with a giant zit in the middle of her forehead.

Actually, that's perfect! Zits are normal for kids our age. And Stella said something about working with nature. What could be more natural than a zit? Oh yeah, I can totally see it. I sit cross-legged on the floor in front of the candle because it feels right. It's like setting the stage. I close my eyes and picture Rachel's face. Eeeuw, that face. And then I imagine the zit. It's enormous. It's right there between her eyes. Man, it is *ugly*. Last of all, I say the words:

On the count of one, the spell's begun.
On the count of two, let the magick
     ring true.
On the count of three, the magick is me.

I get a shiver all down my spine, but I keep holding the image of Rachel's zit for as long as I can. And then I blow out the candle. It's done!

I take a deep breath and look around my room. It looks the same as always. Clothes everywhere, makeup and perfume and stuffies jumbled together on the dresser. Posters on the wall. It's funny because I feel like I just did some actual magick, but there's no proof anywhere. Nothing's changed. Hmph.

Then I think about going to school tomorrow and I start to sniffle. I just *know* it'll be awful. There was this girl in our group in grade six, and she started acting all superior because she was developing so fast. It was like she thought her bra size made her special. Anyway, we all just sort of froze her out. It took a while for her to get it. It was pathetic the way she kept hanging around and calling us.

Finally, she did get it. She left us alone, but then she got so desperate she let me in on her secret, and we still shut her out.

I mean, I didn't tell the others about her uneven boobs, so it wasn't like it made a difference to them. I did the best I could, keeping Rachel's secret for so long. And look how she repaid me. Trying to take Kyle away. She deserved what she got.

But I'm wondering now. Could the freeze-out happen to me? It couldn't, could it? No. My friends would never do that to *me*. By tomorrow, they'll be fine. I should wear something nice tomorrow. Oh! My white pants with the blue blouse. Haley always says the blue brings out my eyes. Where is that top?

I rummage through the clothes on the floor and find it. It's dirty. Of course it is. Why wouldn't it be? Dirty fits right in with the rest of my day. I check my dresser, and the drawers are practically empty. I go downstairs and tell Mom I need some new clothes.

"Lizzie, you don't need any more clothes." Mom rolls her eyes. "You simply need to remember to do your laundry."

I knew she'd say that. I don't know why I thought it might be different this time. "Well, can I go on the computer for a while?"

"Have you done your homework?"

"I wrote the note," I say.

"Lizzie." Mom gives me a look.

"I don't have anything else." I don't tell her that even if I did, it would still be in my locker at school.

She says okay, fine, I can use the computer.

I log in to Facebook and my worst fears are confirmed. None of my friends have sent me a single message. Not one. At least they haven't disappeared from my friends list—yet. But wait, there's a message from someone asking to be added as a friend! That someone is Stella Flowers.

I'm torn. If I add her, I can ask her about the magick. But if she shows up on my list, what will my real friends think?

Real friends? I log out, go to my room, gather my stuffies around me on the bed and cry.

chapter six

Frail hope gets me to school in the morning, hope that my friends will act like everything's fine and hope that Rachel will have a gigantic zit.

My friends aren't gathered under the covered area. Hope number one shattered. Where could they be? We've gathered there every morning since September. Since it's now May, I'd say the change in location was planned. I think maybe I'm going to cry again but no! I refuse to give them the satisfaction. What a fickle bunch of pukes. How dare they?

Just wait until one of them needs to know the latest on hair conditioners. Or where to find their next purse. Or which band is the coolest new thing. I keep on top of that stuff. It's almost spooky how tuned in I am. It's as if I get messages from space. None of them comes close to me on knowing what trend is hot and what's not. They'll come crawling.

I hold my head high and stroll into the school. Home room happens with the blah, blah, blah announcements. It's all normal. I'm good. I check my nails and they're perfect. Next stop, English. Haley's in that class, but I just breeze in and take my seat. I don't even *look* at Haley. I open my books and listen to the teacher. I have no idea what the teacher says, but I listen. Really, I just appear to be listening, but that's good enough.

It's all about appearances.

I can feel Haley looking at me sometimes, actually feel it, but I don't turn toward her.

Not once. They think they can freeze me out? Ha. I'm the queen of freeze.

When lunch hour comes, I don't go to the covered area. I go hunting for Rachel. I don't make the hunt obvious. I walk briskly, like I have some place important to be. I wave and smile at those people I see who aren't in the group but are still okay. Like Mandy, my lab partner.

They wave back. I'm good. I can do this. And then I see someone coming toward me. This person is wearing a lime green hat, the type only grannies wear. What's a granny doing in school? Worse, why is she coming straight at me? And then the granny grins and exposes a mouthful of metal. It's Stella. When she gets closer, she starts to squint. Her face scrunches up, and I think, what? She's going to sneeze on me?

She gets right up in my face and stares.

I back up a step and say, "Uh, what are you doing?"

"Just checking," she says.

"For what?" I ask.

"That girl, Rachel. I don't know her, but I just saw some girls in the washroom all huddled around this one called Rachel. There was some sort of crisis. And then I got a glimpse of Rachel, and she has this huge zit on her forehead. The other girls were trying to help her cover it up with makeup. And then I got a little worried about you."

My grin is probably ten times bigger than the one Stella had. "Are you kidding me?" I squeal.

"Oh no!" Stella says.

"What?"

She frowns and gets in my face again. "You didn't, did you?"

I back away and say, "Would you stop that? And what didn't I do?"

"You didn't cast a spell to give her a zit, did you?" Stella asks.

"So what if I did?" I shake my head. "I really didn't think it would work. But it must have! Do you have any idea how amazing this is? Which bathroom were they in? I've got to see this."

Stella takes a deep breath and says, "I think there's something else you've got to see."

"Oh no," I say. "Nothing will beat the zit. It's prime." And then I notice a faint pulsing in my forehead. What is that? I put my hand over it and rub, and the skin hurts. "Ow! What the heck?"

"Hurry," Stella whispers. "We've got to go for cover."

"What do you mean?" I ask.

Stella grabs hold of my arm and tugs. "Come on, Lizzie." She glances at my forehead and her eyes widen. "Let's go!" And then she pulls me down the hall, practically galloping in her big brown shoes.

"Jeez," I complain. "Slow down. Where's the fire?" But as soon as the words are out of my mouth, I know where the fire is. It's on my forehead. And it's getting hotter every second.

We burst into the first bathroom we find. A couple of girls are combing their hair at the mirror, and Stella yells, "Clear out! She's going to be sick!"

The girls grab their purses and run. They don't look back.

"I'll hold the door," Stella says. "You, uh, better check the mirror."

I'm afraid to look. I have to look. And when I do..."OH MY GOD!"

It's unbelievable. It's grotesque. *They're* grotesque. Blossoming on my forehead are not one but *three* enormous zits. I grab hold of a sink to keep myself from collapsing. I've never seen anything like it. I swear the zits are growing before my eyes. "This...I...you..."

The ability to form words leaves me. Until now, I was one of the chosen few who never got zits. Never. My skin has remained smooth and pure as a baby's. It's as gorgeous as my hair.

"I told you, Lizzie," Stella whispers. "The Law of Three. Remember?"

Into the fog of my mind comes a memory. Something about magick coming back threefold. I'd completely forgotten that. "It's a *law*?"

Stella nods. "Big time."

I feel myself blinking but not to stop tears. It's more like I'm in shock. Yes, I'm in shock, like someone who's just been in a car accident. I can't think, I can only blink. And then a thought does come. It's this. RUN! I look around. Way up high on the cement wall is a tiny window.

"Quick," I say, "come and stand by this wall."

"Why?" Stella asks.

"So I can get on your shoulders and reach the window."

"I don't think so." Stella shakes her head. "These windows don't open."

"How do you know?" I ask.

She shrugs. "I've tried them."

She tried them? Just how weird is this kid? There's no time to worry about that now. Instead I ask, "Couldn't you just, you know, make a spell to open it?"

"No." Stella laughs. Actually laughs. "I don't have that kind of power. My gift is more about finding the talent in others. Like you. Only I didn't expect quite *this* much from you." She laughs again.

I put my hands on my hips. "This is not funny. You got me into this mess. Now how am I going to get out?"

"I got you into this?" she asks.

"Yes! You taught me that stupid spell, didn't you?"

She shrugs. "True. But I also told you magick isn't a game, and I warned you about how it comes back threefold."

She's right. She did tell me that. But that's beside the point. I still need to escape—unseen. "You wouldn't by any chance have a spell to make me invisible, would you?"

"Sorry. Can't do that either. But I can do something." She takes the hideous green granny hat off her head and sticks it on mine. "There. Look at that. If you pull it low over your forehead, no one will see the zits. Poof! They're invisible."

I stare at her. She has seriously bad hat hair. It's flat on top and then all those frizzy curls form a right angle at her ears and totally go their own way. I might feel sorry for her if I didn't have bigger problems.

Slowly, I turn and look into the mirror. And it's really, really weird because the hat actually looks sort of okay. Maybe even better than okay. It might even look good. "Wow," I murmur, "this is my kind of magick."

"Isn't it great?" Stella smiles. "It's my baba's. She loaned it to me."

Her baba's? As in the old-school witch? I'm not going there. I can't. I just nod and say, "I guess it's better than nothing."

I look at her and am shocked again by her hair. "Do you have a hairbrush?"

She digs in her backpack and comes up with a ratty old red brush. She holds it out toward me and says, "Here you go."

"Um. Thanks. But I was just noticing you have, like, total hat hair."

"Really?" Stella glances in the mirror, then starts yanking the brush through her hair. The flattened area revives and blends with the mass. "Thanks for telling me, Lizzie. I never would have noticed."

The bell sounds and we both startle. I look in the mirror to double-check that the zits are covered. They are. I can still feel them, but so long as they're hidden, it's okay. I tilt my head and ask, "This hat doesn't make me look gangsta, does it?"

"Oh no," Stella says. "My baba would never go for that. She's really cute."

Some people have no idea. Note to self: Do not trust Stella's opinions on cuteness. "Okay, I guess we're good to go. I'll go first."

"What do you mean?" Stella asks.

I take hold of the door handle, "Uh, we can't be seen leaving together, can we?"

Stella gets a funny look, but that's just her, the way she is, right?

chapter seven

Science class is not as horrible as I thought it would be. I think it's mainly because Mandy is jealous of my hat. "That hat is so dope, Lizzie. Where did you get it?"

I shrug. "Oh, I can't remember. Must have been somewhere in the mall."

Mr. Sparks asks if I have something for him. For one horrible second, I think he wants the hat. And then I remember the apology letter. I take it out of my purse and hand it to him with a smile.

He says, "Hmph. Fine. You can report for detention today in room 101."

"Um," I say, "how long do I have to do this? Until the end of the week, right?" It's Thursday and I'm really hoping he'll mess up on the details.

He shakes his head. "Lizzie, I hope some day you'll decide to put that brain of yours to better use. Your final day of detention will be next Wednesday." And he walks away.

"Jeez," says Mandy, "that was sort of rude."

"For sure," I say. But it occurs to me that the best way to keep *not* looking at Kyle is to pretend I'm doing the lab work. "So, uh, what are we supposed to be doing here?" I ask.

"I wonder about that all the time," Mandy says. "I mean, are we supposed to follow our own path or just let fate decide what happens?"

Omigod. She is so stunned. I look over at the next table to see what the science geeks are doing. I catch them looking at me and whispering. I give them the stare down, and they quickly turn away. Do they actually think I was trying to cheat yesterday? Is that why they would dare to stare at me, Lizzie Lane? And then, very clearly, I hear one of them say, "It *is* Stella's."

Oh, wow. The geeks must recognize the hat. I take a deep breath. Okay, it doesn't matter. Their opinion doesn't count, does it? I mean, they might know Stella and her hat, but who are they going to tell? No one that matters.

The zits start itching, and I can't do a thing about it. I'm going to go crazy. "Quick," I say to Mandy, "get out your textbook."

"For real?" she asks.

"Yes. We must be past the mucus by now so it'll be fine. We can do it."

Mandy hauls her textbook out of her backpack and starts flipping through the pages. I look at the blackboard, and there are actual instructions for doing a lab with a simple saltwater solution. I can handle that. So we do the experiment. It doesn't turn out right, but the class is over way faster than normal.

Room 101 is like a dungeon. It's a stinky little room behind the gym. I swear the heat vents must blow air directly from the boys' locker room. The teacher supervising is this withered old dude with a permanent mean mug. I think he's been in the dungeon forever, and the fumes have poisoned him. He asks for my name, then points to a sign that says *SILENCE!*

Then he points to a chair. I sit in the chair and look around. I don't know any of the kids in there. I go back up to the teacher and ask, "How long *is* detention, anyway? Fifteen minutes?"

He smiles at me. It's really awful because his teeth are yellow and his lips go super thin and I can see his gums. "One hour."

I feel like I've been shot. There's pain in my gut and my knees practically buckle. An entire hour in here? I'll die. I go back to the table and put my head on my arms. How did this happen to me?

Rachel. She did this. One giant zit is nowhere near enough to get back at her. I need something bigger, something huge and life changing. As in, she gets kidnapped and dropped in the jungle. In a pool of crocodiles. Naked. No, wait. She wakes up to find herself standing naked in front of a school assembly. All one thousand students are there and they have rotten tomatoes to throw...

A sound from the door disturbs my lovely train of thought, and I look up. There's Stella! I'm actually happy to see her. I wave my fingers and she gives me a tiny smile. She finishes checking in with Mr. Mean and then she sits down beside me.

"Why are you here?" I whisper.

Mean is on us in a flash. "Silence! If I hear one more sound, your detention will be extended by thirty minutes."

He is an evil, evil man.

Stella slides me a note. It says: *I came to see you.*

I look at her, and she seems serious. Who would go into the dungeon to visit a prisoner? I write back: *Why?*

She shrugs, then writes: *I need to get the hat back.*

My look gives her an answer, and she hastily writes: *Not right now. After.*

Whew.

Then she writes: *I can teach you some magick while we're here.*

OK.

She nods and writes: *You have to be careful what you wish for.*

I write: *Duh.*

Stella grins and jots: *Like attracts like.*

What's that supposed to mean? I write.

She scribbles: *It means that what you put out there is what will come back to you.*

The zits on my forehead throb, and I sigh. *So this is useless for getting back at Rachel. Let's just forget it.*

She shakes her head. *There is a way. But first, let's try something else.* She puts her hand into her pocket, pulls out a small stone and gives it to me. It's golden orange, almost clear, with swirls of darker color inside.

Stella writes: *This is amber. It'll help get rid of your zits.*

I raise my brows. *For real?*

She nods, then starts digging in her purse. This time she pulls out a bandage and writes: *Use this to stick the amber on your forehead.*

I stare at her.

She nods vigorously.

When I don't make a move to take the bandage, she writes: *No one will notice. The hat will hide it. You just have to believe and it will work.*

Right. I just have to believe. Do I believe? Not. But then, what about the zits? They sure seem like solid proof. I eye the bandage. Maybe if I stick the amber to the bandage I can tilt the hat back just long enough to slap the amber on in one fast move? I cast a nervous glance around the room. No one is watching us. Most of them look like they're asleep. One guy even has his mouth hanging open and a tiny trail of drool is leaking out the side. And I'm worried about sticking a rock on my forehead in front of these people?

Wait a minute. Sticking a rock on my forehead is definitely weirder than drooling. I am so torn about what to do. There are no simple solutions.

Stella reaches into her backpack and pulls out a large textbook. She stands it up on the table in front of me and *voila*! I have cover.

I take a deep breath. I can do this. I tear open the bandage wrapper. I place the amber on the bandage. I crouch low behind the book. I place my left hand on the brim of the hat and hold the amber bandage unit in my right. One, two, three...

I push on the hat with my left, and it snags on a zit. This glitch throws me off and my right hand wobbles. The amber goes flying. As I try to grab it, the hat bumps the book and knocks it over. I look up and there, just walking through the door, is Kyle. Our eyes meet. His widen in shock.

It's more than shock. It's horror. He gasps. Stella gasps. Mr. Mean rotates his head toward me and *he* gasps. Gasping sounds come from every corner of the room. Maybe even retching sounds.

"Oh my," says Mr. Mean. "You, ah, may be excused. Perhaps your friend there will take you to the nurse. Hurry, now."

What's happened? Have the zits grown to such humungous size that I now look like a monster? I yank the hat down low, grab my purse and flee. I can hear Stella running behind me. There's no mistaking the sound of those shoes, but I don't look back.

chapter eight

By the time I'm almost home, I know what I have to do. It's crystal clear. I have to leave the country. When I show Mom my face, I'm sure she'll agree. I feel a sob gathering in my throat as I wonder if she'll come with me. But what if I scare her too?

This whole time, Stella has been following me. I'm pretending she doesn't exist, but she's not getting it. She keeps saying stuff like, "It's not *that* bad. I found the amber. We can heal it. Please listen to me, Lizzie."

At last, with one foot on my front lawn, I turn to her and say, "I never want to see you again. Got that?"

She nods and says, "I understand. But I do feel somewhat responsible for all this. I want to make it right. If we ask, I'm sure my baba will cure your zits. I'm only trying to help."

"Your kind of help I can do without."

"But what are you going to do?" she asks. "Those zits...you could have them for weeks."

She's right. I could leave the country, but the zits would go with me. I should get her baba to fix them and *then* leave the country. I glare at Stella. "Are you *sure* your baba can fix this?"

She bites her lip. "I'm almost sure. If she takes a look, she can tell you. She should be home right now."

I take a deep breath. What have I got to lose? I shrug and say, "Fine. I'll give you one last chance. Let's go."

Stella's house looks like every other house on the street from the outside. It's pretty average on the inside too, until we hit the kitchen. Walking in there is like stumbling upon a vegetable war. Not only is the floor lettuce green, the walls are radish red and the cupboards are carrot orange. Plus, there are actual plants everywhere. Bundles of plant matter hang from ceiling. Bowls overflow. Garlands of garlic are draped over the windows. And then I see her—Baba. Standing at the stove is a tiny old woman wearing a polka-dot apron, a flowered dress and an enormous hat. A bunch of plants are sticking out of the hat. It's like she's camouflaged in there.

"Ah, Stella!" she says. "You've brought a friend. How nice!"

"Hi, Baba," Stella says. "This is Lizzie. From next door." She tosses a quick look in my direction and adds, "The one I told you about, remember?"

The baba's eyes narrow. She lifts a long bony finger and points it at me. "This is her?"

I laugh. I can't help it. "Yes. Ha ha. It's me."

"And you're wearing my hat," the baba says. "Why?"

"Oh! Ha-ha. Just because." I have to get out of here.

I start backing up, and a totally creepy voice says, "I see through your clothes."

I open my mouth to shriek, but something more like a squawk comes out. And the voice squawks back.

"Oh, honestly, Angela," the baba says, "how many times have I told you not to say that to guests?"

Stella reaches up into a tall plant and when she pulls back, a glossy green parrot is perched on her arm. "This is Angela," she says. "Say hello, Angela."

The parrot remains silent.

Stella rolls her eyes. "She's just being difficult."

"True," says the baba. "But I have a feeling there's more difficulty here than her." She eyes me and asks, "The hat? Are you hiding something?"

She's sharp, I'll give her that. I look at Stella and she nods. I remove the hat.

The baba slaps a hand to her breast and whispers, "Holy Mother Earth! What have you done, child?"

In a small voice, Stella says, "It's my fault. I told her how to cast a spell. But I didn't explain the laws properly. Can you fix it?"

The baba clucks her tongue and says something like, "Ay yi yi!" She steps closer to me, squints at my forehead and closes her eyes. "This," she says, "is very bad. I haven't seen pox like these for many years."

"Pox?" I ask. The very word sounds scary. "What are pox?"

"No, Baba," Stella says. "They're just zits. Pimples. Blemishes."

The baba narrows her gaze. "You are certain?"

"I, um, gave one zit to another girl," I say. "I didn't ask for her to get pox."

"I see." The baba purses her lips, studies me again, then says, "Sit. There." She points to a chair beside a small round table. I sit.

She starts mumbling in some strange language, and I think, Okay, good, she's casting the reverse spell. But then she grabs a towel from a drawer, dips it into a pot on the stove, wrings it out and hands it to me. "Put this on your forehead," she says.

"That's it?" I ask. "I put this on and it's all better?"

She laughs. "Don't be silly. That's just some Epsom salts and calendula oil. I was going to soak my feet, but you go ahead. It'll help draw the pus."

I almost gag. "Pus?"

"You haven't seen these zits recently?" she asks.

"Not for a few hours."

The baba does the clucking thing again. "Perhaps it's better that you don't look. Put on the towel."

I put on the towel. It stings at first, but the baba says, "Hold it there!" I hold it. After a moment, it actually feels soothing.

"Now," says the baba, "what spell did you use?"

I tell her and she looks impressed. "It's possible my Stella was right about you. She told me yesterday that she felt something in your aura and I agree. You must have some natural ability to get those results from a simple spell. And on your first try."

"Uh. Thanks," I say.

She sniffs. "Not that it's any help to me. Sometimes the simplest spells are the hardest to reverse." She stands still for a moment, plainly thinking.

I doubt this is a good sign. I mean if she has to think about it, does she really know what she's doing?

"Yes," she says, "I know what we'll do." She looks at me and smiles. I get this eerie feeling that she heard my thoughts. Of course, that's not possible.

"Stella, I would like you to assist. Let's gather together. Quickly now." The baba claps her hands and Stella leaps into action. She places two more chairs at the table, then lights the fat candle that sits in the center. They both take a seat and join hands.

"Just a minute," says the baba. She gets up and fetches a length of string. "We'll need your hands too," she says to me.

And she ties the string around the towel, cinching it firmly to my head.

Wow. If my friends could see me now... I banish the thought. *Banish.* There's a nice magickal word.

The baba sits again, and this time we all join hands. The baba says, "We will all picture Lizzie's forehead being healed and smooth. And the other girl? What is her name?"

"Um," I mutter, "Rachel."

The baba says, "Rachel's forehead too. Perfectly smooth."

"But–," I say.

"No buts! It's the only way. Now hold the images while we chant. You join in as soon as you can, Lizzie." Then in soft voices, she and Stella start off.

Raise the Wind and Earth,
Raise the Water and Fire,
Raise the power ever higher.

Their voices get louder, and they repeat the chant. And again, louder still. I get it and join in. We repeat the chant several more times, and I try very hard to picture my perfect forehead. It's harder to picture Rachel being healed, but since it's the only way, I do that too.

All at once, the baba drops our hands and gets to her feet. She raises her arms in the air and intones:

Girls will be girls and play their games.
They'll call up zits and call out names.
Let the lessons they learn from all
*   that's been said,*
Be written on their heart instead of
*   their head.*

She looks at me and Stella. "Would you ladies like some tea and cake? I'm famished."

"Yes, thanks, Baba," Stella says.

"Um," I mutter, "is that it?"

The baba pauses in filling a kettle and looks at me. "That all depends on you."

"On me?"

"Yes," she says. "You must write the lesson of the zit on your heart."

Omigod. This is a bust. The baba is crazed. A zit lesson on my heart? I'm too numb to stand so I drink tea and eat cake. Stella and her baba chat, and I have no idea what they say.

When I finally get up to leave, the baba says, "Wait. I have something for you." She bustles out of the room and returns with another granny hat, a purple one. "Take it."

"Oh," I say, "I couldn't. Really."

"You must," she says. "Purple is the color of magickal mastery. More importantly, it's the color of spirituality. You need it."

"You wouldn't happen to have something in blue, would you?" I ask.

She frowns. "You weren't listening. I said you need the purple. Put it on now, and then you must go and meditate."

I blink at her. "I don't know what you mean."

The baba turns to Stella. "You didn't instruct her to consider the higher self?"

Stella flushes pink and shakes her head. "Sorry, Baba."

"Ay yi yi!" says the baba. She levels a finger at Stella. "You were far too hasty."

"I was only trying to help her," Stella says.

The baba's face softens. "I know, child. And I agree, it's plain that she needs it. So you must tell her more or she will be stuck in this muck."

I have to get out of there, even if I have to take Stella with me. I rip off the towel, plop the purple hat on my head and say, "Let's go."

Just before the door closes behind us, I hear Angela say, "I see through your clothes."

chapter nine

We book it across our front yards and into my house. I run for the nearest mirror and whip off the hat. And there are three zits—fairly ordinary zits.

Stella comes up behind me and says, "Wow! They're a lot better, huh?"

I'm torn. On the one hand, I do not have giant pus-filled pox on my forehead. I shudder. I can't bear to imagine what they must have looked like. On the other hand... "But I still have zits. I want them *gone*."

Stella shrugs. "That's where it's up to you. Remember what my baba said?"

Right. I'm supposed to write lessons on my heart and meditate. As if. I take one last look at the zits and turn to Stella. "All I wanted to do was get back at Rachel. All of this"—I wave a hand in the air—"this mumbo jumbo, it's way too complicated. I mean, it might be worth it if we could do other stuff, like make a love potion."

I stop talking and consider this. A love potion would be good. If I could give one to Kyle then he'd fall in love with me and forget all about the zits. And then I could just dump him. See how he likes that!

"Lizzie," Stella says, "do you want me to explain the perfect revenge spell?"

"Whatever," I say. "Let's go to my room. I need to lie down."

We get comfy in my room, me on the bed and Stella on the floor, and she says, "Okay. I think you understand the Law of Three, right?"

I give her a look.

"Right," she says. "So clearly it's dangerous to use magick for revenge if you try to hurt the other person."

"I've got to tell you, Stella," I say, "the whole *point* of revenge is to hurt the other person."

"Yes. So what you do is give them something that's good that will actually mess them up."

I shake my head. "You're not making any sense."

"No?" she asks. "Think about it. Let's say there's a jerk that goes around breaking stuff just for the fun of it. You know, he kicks over people's fences. Or he wrecks the playground equipment at the park. He sets trees on fire. And his buddies think he's cool for doing it."

"I don't know any idiots like *that*," I say.

"But if you did. What could you do to him to change his ways without hurting yourself?"

"I could...um...Oh, I know, I'd get him to catch himself on fire...No! Wait. Uh...

Jeez." I glare at Stella. "I couldn't do any magick to him without getting hurt."

"What if you gave him love of order and harmony?" Stella glances around my messy room and grins. "That wouldn't hurt you, would it?"

"Hey!" I say. But as I consider what she said, I can't help grinning back. "So he wouldn't want to wreck stuff anymore, right? And all his loser friends would think he was a straight-edge dork. And they'd ditch him?"

Stella shrugs, but there's a wicked sparkle in her eyes. "I think you're getting the idea."

"Oooh," I croon. "I'm liking this. A lot."

"So now," Stella says, "you just have to figure out which trait to give Rachel that would mess her up. And not hurt you."

"Right! Okay. Let's see. Rachel is a snob. She's shallow. She doesn't care about anyone but herself. She'll do whatever it takes to get what she wants. She's a drama queen, and she thinks she's all that. And she's sneaky."

"Sounds pretty bad," Stella says. "I'm surprised she has any friends."

"Me too," I say.

"So how can you change her enough to make a difference?"

"I don't know. I'd probably have to do, like, fifty spells to totally whack her," I say.

Stella laughs. "Maybe. But for now, what's one thing you could do that would get her in trouble?"

"This is hard," I whine.

"I told you it was tricky," Stella says. "But it can be done. My Baba said it's important to think about the other person's higher self."

"I'm not getting that part," I say.

"The higher self is like the person's life force, or their spirit. All life is supposed to be naturally in tune with all other life. So when people are mean or evil, it's not their spirit that's doing it. It's just their ignorance."

I blink at her. "Really?"

She nods vigorously. "Really. Even people like Rachel have a life force."

"Well, yeah," I say. "If she didn't, she'd be dead."

Stella tilts her head and says, "Actually, just her body would be dead. Her spirit would live on in another realm."

I hear the sound of the front door opening, and Mom calls, "Lizzie? Are you home?"

"Great," I say. "Just great. I totally forgot I was going to ask my mom to get me out of the country. Only now, if I show her these pathetic zits, she won't believe they're a big deal, will she?" I glare at Stella. "I thought we were going to finish getting rid of my zits here?"

Stella sighs. "Tell you what. You meditate for a while, and then I'll come back over later and we'll see what we can do."

"Stella?"

"Yeah?"

"I have no idea how to meditate," I say. "I'm not even sure what that is. Does it have something to do with yoga?"

"Lizzie?" Mom calls.

"Just a minute," I yell back.

"Yoga?" Stella asks.

"My mom did yoga," I say, "and she said something about meditating at class. I don't know any yoga."

Stella says, "I don't know about yoga, but all I do when I meditate is breathe and focus on high thoughts."

"You're kidding, right?" I ask.

Stella shakes her head.

"All righty, then," I say. "I guess we'll see what we can do later."

As soon as Stella is out the door, I say to my mom, "I need to go to a dermatologist. Now. It's an emergency."

Mom laughs. "Lizzie, dear, your blemishes are perfectly normal. They're caused by hormones. Don't worry, they'll probably be gone within a few days, a week at most."

Omigod. She is so cold. She used to love me. I go back to my room and put on the purple hat. It does hide the zits. And it doesn't look too bad. It actually has some style with its flirty little brim and a small lilac flower on one side. I wonder where Stella's baba gets her hats?

chapter ten

When Stella shows up later, I ask her about the hats.

"I think Baba gets them at the Thrift Store," Stella says.

"You mean, they're *used*?" I ask.

"Probably." She shrugs. "So how did the meditation go?"

"Oh, that," I say. "I forgot to do it. Sorry. Should we do it now?"

She nods. "I brought some incense we can light. I find it helps."

"How long does this take?" I ask.

"Not long. Maybe ten minutes. It's hard to stay focused for longer when you're not used to it."

I don't tell her that ten minutes seems way too long. Three would be plenty, but I'm learning that nothing happens instantly in magick. Stella lights the incense and it smells okay, sort of woodsy and flowery. I could probably just spray perfume if I decide to get into this on a regular basis.

"Now sit down, cross-legged, and get comfortable," Stella says. "Close your eyes and focus on a mantra."

"A what?"

"A little saying," she says. "The one I use is 'I am light and peace.' I just say it in my head, over and over."

"I am light and peace?" I repeat. How goofy is that?

"That's it," Stella nods. "And if you find your thoughts wandering, just bring yourself back to that and keep repeating it. The only other thoughts you might allow are creative ideas about the quality you're going to give Rachel."

This is so lame. I am *not* going to be doing it on a regular basis. We sit there with our eyes closed, and I think, *I am light and peace*, and then I wonder about checking in on Facebook. Wow, the past couple days have been strange. I can't believe I didn't remember to check it earlier.

I am light and peace. As if. My foot has a terrible itch, and I scratch it. *I am light and peace.* That casserole Mom made for dinner was gross. Now my back is itchy. I look at the alarm clock by my bed and not even two minutes have passed. And can I really handle wearing a used hat? I'm wearing it right now, aren't I? That was part of the deal. Wear the purple hat for magickal mastery and spirituality. Whatever.

I've hardly ever thought about spirituality. I mean, what's it for? *I am light and peace.* Like that's going to help anything. It's going to get rid of zits? I don't think so. And it's not as if saying it is going to make it true. But what if it did? *I am light and peace.*

That's actually sort of nice. For sure the light part is good. I don't ever want to be overweight. Darn, I think my foot is going to sleep. I hate that. I shift around and take a peek at Stella. There she is with her eyes closed, her wild jumble of hair, her scrawny body. Omigod.

"Psst! Stella!" I hiss.

She opens her eyes.

"Don't say that part about the light," I tell her. "You're way too skinny already."

She blinks a few times. Then she just falls over on the floor and starts shaking.

"What's wrong?" I ask. "You're not having a seizure or something, are you?"

"I'm fine," she gasps. "Omigod, Lizzie. You are unbelievable." And she goes into this spasm of laughter. It's like she's totally lost it. When she can talk again, she says, "I can't wait to tell Baba you said that. She's going to love it."

In my coldest voice, I ask, "What did I say?"

"Being light," she snorts, "means that I'm skinny."

"You *are*," I tell her.

"Yeah," she says, "I know. Only the light I'm focusing on is spiritual, not physical."

"Well fine," I sputter. "But maybe it's like you said, all life is in tune. And your body's been listening in. What about that?"

Stella's jaw drops. "Whoa! I never thought of that."

I cross my arms over my chest. "Maybe you should."

"I think you're right," she says. "And I really do think you have a natural talent for magick. I don't know what you've been doing with it before now."

"I have a talent for picking hot trends," I tell her.

She nods. "That makes sense. The universe can have a quirky sense of humor, and you do relate to things in a totally quirky way."

"Are you saying *I'm* quirky?" I ask.

She grins. "Maybe."

Wow. She has so much to learn.

"All right," Stella says, "let's get on with the Rachel revenge. What have you got?"

I don't have anything, but I'm not about to admit it. My brain scrambles through the possibilities. I'm sure there aren't any good things I could give her that I don't already have, so I'm not worried about the law of three. So what then? I could give her honesty, but it's too late for that. I could give her generosity so *she'd* give stuff to others, but her friends wouldn't hate that. And then I've got it!

"What's that called, when you feel sorry for other people?" I ask.

"Sympathy?"

I shake my head. "No, that other word. It's like when you don't just feel sorry for them, you feel how bad they feel yourself."

"Ah!" Stella smiles. "Empathy."

"That's it! She needs to feel for others. Then she'd know what it's like when she's a snob and ignores people. Or when she trashes others to get her way. She'd even feel bad about what she did to me. Maybe even bad enough to confess."

"You never know," Stella says.

I go on. "Did I tell you how she's always

making fun of other people's clothes and hair and stuff? I've heard her. And all her stupid little so-called friends just love it. They laugh at everything she says. If she couldn't do that anymore, they'd think she was just a huge bore. For sure, they'd ditch her. She is going to be so screwed."

Stella nods. "You know, I think you've got it. It's perfect."

"It *is* perfect, isn't it?" I say. "So how do we do it?"

"I can't help you with the actual spell casting. But I'll write down the words, and then you do it almost the same way you did the first one. Light a candle and sit before it. Focus on Rachel and her higher self. Then speak the spell and visualize her in the light of the candle flame for a short time. After you've done that, you blow out the candle, and it's done."

I find a pen and a sheet of paper and hand them to Stella. She writes down some words while I try to decide if Rachel has a higher self. I guess the fact that she's alive must mean something.

Stella finishes writing and says, "Try to memorize the words before you cast the spell." Then she fishes around in her pocket, pulls out another rock and gives it to me.

I'm a little wary of rocks, considering what happened with the amber, but I take it. It's smooth and whitish grey with a pearly sheen. "What is it?"

"It's a moonstone. For luck and for connecting with your intuition."

"Thanks," I say. Considering how good I am at intuition already, I doubt I need a rock for that. But luck, that I could use.

After she leaves, I memorize the spell and then set the stage. I put on the purple hat. I light the candle and place the moonstone beside it on the table. I sit on the floor and stare into the flame. Finally, in that sing-song voice Stella's baba used, I intone:

Upon the planes in which I live,
The gift of empathy I now give,
To Rachel with all my heart and soul,

To change her and to make her whole.
By all on high and Law of Three,
This is my will, so shall it be.

I focus on the light of the candle and see Rachel there. I really see her. And then I blow out the candle and that's that. Done.

I check the mirror, and the zits are still there. I'm not surprised. This means I need two plans for tomorrow. Plan A is when I wake up in the morning, zit free, and am able to go to school. Plan B means the zits live on and there's no chance I will go anywhere. I'll have to pretend I'm sick, but I can do that.

Back to Plan A. The largest question is, do I wear the purple hat to school or not? If I go hatless and show everyone (Kyle) that my forehead is clear, they'll wonder what they saw in room 101. I could say the zits were fake, makeup artistry to get out of detention. That's quite good.

But if I wear the hat again, people will probably point and whisper stuff like, "Do you know why she's wearing that? It's cuz she's hiding a cluster of volcanic zits." And at that point, it would be fun to whip off the hat and be all cool. The rumor spreaders would look like idiots, wouldn't they? It would serve them right. Yes, I'll definitely wear the hat.

All at once, I'm super tired. Small wonder, considering the day I've had. I'm so tired, I can't even bring myself to log in to Facebook. It's all I can do to brush my teeth before I crash into bed.

chapter eleven

It's like magick! No, it's not *like* magick, it *is* magick. I am zit free! No matter which way I tilt my head, I can't see anything marring my perfect forehead.

I get dressed as fast as I can. I can't wait to get to school. Because if I'm zit-less, then that must mean the revenge spell worked. And I get to watch Rachel's world fall apart. Yes!

No.

Huh?

I try that thought again. I get to watch Rachel suffer the way she made me suffer. Eeeuw. What the heck? I should be happy about getting what I want, shouldn't I? That's how it's supposed to work. I wonder if the zits have reversed and poisoned my brain? And then I get another thought, a brand new one. And it's one I should have had a lot sooner.

I'm going to feel the pain of others.

Omigod. What have I done? This is so *not* good. I grab my purse, slap the purple hat on my head and bolt out the front door. I go next door, stand on the lawn and yell, "Stellaaaaa! I need to talk to you!"

And Stella comes out of her house. She's wearing neon pink pants with a lemon yellow top and bright red shoes. To top it off, she's wearing the hat her baba wore yesterday, the one with bunches of plants sticking out everywhere. I'm so stunned that I forget what I was going to say.

"Hi, Lizzie," Stella says. "What's wrong?"

"Um," I say. What if I tell her that she's totally destroyed my life and I hate her? I can't do it. Her feelings would be hurt. So I say, "My zits are gone."

She grins. "Good for you, Lizzie. You did it!"

We start walking toward the school, and I wonder what people will think seeing us together, but I can't tell Stella to pretend she doesn't know me, can I?

So I try to tell her my problem. "Stella, there's a glitch in the revenge spell. It's like this. I don't want to see Rachel get hurt. I mean I do, that was the whole point, but now I feel sorry for her."

Stella gives me a sideways look. "Uh-oh. We, uh, didn't think about that, did we?"

"I know *I* didn't!" I say. "I was sure I couldn't give her something good that I didn't already have. I mean, I think I've always cared about other people. I'm sure I did. But this isn't like that. And it's really scary because I got a triple whammy, right? Now I can't even *think* about other people getting hurt. It makes my stomach feel icky."

"Really?" Stella asks.

"Really. So we're going to have to get your baba to fix this too, okay?"

Stella frowns. "I don't know if she'll fix this one."

"Why not?" I ask.

"Because..."

Before Stella can finish what she was saying, a kid on a bike zooms past and grabs her hat.

Stella yells, "Hey!" But the kid just laughs. And then he throws her hat onto the street. A car drives right over it.

Stella's face crumples. "That was Baba's favorite hat!"

Tears well up in my eyes, and I put my arm around her. "You poor dear."

I can't believe I said that, but I did. And then I say, "Here. You take the purple one." So much for doing my hat trick later. Doesn't matter. For some reason, it's lost its appeal. Stella says, "Thanks, Lizzie. But you keep it. It looks really cute on you."

I can't tell her that's not comforting. I mean, considering she said her baba was cute and her taste in clothes...Oh, so what if she wears goofy clothes? Doesn't hurt anybody, does it?

I feel like I've entered an alternate universe. My mind is warped. I don't understand half the things I'm thinking. Okay, I do understand them, but they're not me.

It gets worse.

We arrive at school, and out of habit I go by way of the covered area. All my friends are there again. They take one look at me and Stella and crack up. They don't even have the decency to hide their laughter. Poor things. They're only doing it because it makes them feel superior. I know.

I stop and say, "Hi. How's it going?"

Their laughter cuts out and they start looking at each other. They're searching for clues on how to react. I wasn't supposed to stop. I was supposed to ignore them and pretend I wasn't hurt by their laughter. Key word, *pretend*. Talk about stupid games.

Finally, Haley says, "Some hat, Lizzie. Any special reason you're wearing it?"

I glance at Stella and grin. "Stella says it looks cute on me." All right! I can still have fun!

"That's not what I heard," Haley says. She smirks at the other girls and they smirk back.

"Really? Hmmm. Maybe we shouldn't believe everything we hear." I take off the hat and say, "Then again, sometimes people are telling the truth. And even their friends don't believe them."

Their seeking eyes don't bother me. I know they're trying to work it out, the rumored zits and the lack of evidence. Nothing is adding up for them.

"Lizzie," one of the girls says, "do you happen to know where I can get something for my, um, skin?" Poor thing. She's prone to breaking out.

"Actually," I say, "I don't. But I'll check on that for you."

She smiles. "Really? You'd do that for me, after...?" She stops.

"No problem," I say. "Catch you later. Come on, Stella. We don't want to be late. It upsets the teachers."

Stella and I meet up again at lunchtime and she says, "It's kind of strange. I've noticed about five other girls are wearing hats today."

I grin at her. "That's because they saw me wearing a hat yesterday. Lizzie Lane is a trendsetter—the one to watch."

It's a relief to know that some things haven't changed. We decide to go searching for Rachel. We find her in the same washroom Stella saw her in yesterday. She's gathered with her little group, and they're all looking bored.

At least, they look bored until Stella and I walk in. Then their eyes gleam and they turn eagerly to Rachel.

Rachel says, "Oh. Hi, Lizzie. And whoever you are."

"This is Stella," I say.

"Hi, Stella," Rachel says. "Nice to meet you."

The other girls' heads swivel back and forth. They're waiting for Rachel to skewer me or go after Stella's clothes. There's an easy mark. But Rachel disappoints them.

In fact, she can barely look at me. The silence in the room is thick.

I can't stand it. I decide to help her out. "So, Rachel. No hard feelings, eh?"

Her eyes widen and she slaps a hand over her mouth.

"No, seriously. I mean it." And I do mean it, so I add, "Don't worry about it, okay? We're even. I'm fine."

She bursts into tears and throws her arms around me. "I'm so sorry, Lizzie! I can't imagine how horrible it must have been for you. So humiliating! And now, room 101? Waahhh."

I feel awful, but I manage to pat her back. "It's okay. Although room 101 really is horrible. It's like death in there."

Rachel emits another sob, and I cringe. Jeez, what's up with that? I can't even rub it in about how much I'm suffering? Sick. I sigh and say, "But I only have to go there four more times."

"Still," Rachel sniffles, "I had to go there once. And the teacher in charge is such a turd..." She flinches. "I mean, the poor old guy. I guess he's been stuck down there forever."

I get a little teary-eyed myself over Mr. Mean. *Ouch*! Okay, so it's really Mr. Snead. I knew that. "For sure, it must be awful for him being there every day. The smell down there is so disgusting."

"Maybe," Rachel says, "we should get him a fan."

"Yeah! Or some flowers or incense or something." I look at Stella. "You know where to get incense, right?"

Stella grins. "For sure. I might even have some in my backpack." She starts digging around and comes up with a little cone-shaped lump.

"Um," one of the watchers says, "I think we're gonna go now."

"Yeah," says another. "This is, like, really weird."

Rachel looks like I feel. Stricken. Together we say, "Sorry!"

"Really," I add, "we didn't mean to bother you. Are you going to be all right?"

They stare at me. Slowly, they nod and start backing away. As they escape out the door, I hear one say, "Man! That was so totally freaky!"

I guess it was. Either that or magickal.

chapter twelve

Science class. Kyle. I walk in and look straight at him. He is so hot. But clearly, he's also shallow. I mean, he gets turned off of Rachel because he hears a rumor about her? And now he can't even look at me because I had zits?

Or is that because he thinks I'm a cheater? Rachel offered to tell everyone that she gave me the exam key, and I was tempted. But then I thought about how much that could hurt her, and I felt sick.

I told her to forget it. I couldn't handle it. I have to protect myself, right?

Only then she said, "But Lizzie, I'll feel better if I tell the truth."

It's all very confusing. Things were much simpler when we only cared about ourselves. Like Kyle. I look at him again, and I even feel sorry for him. Poor guy, it must be hard trying to keep up that image.

He glances up and catches my eye. I can't resist. I whip off the purple hat. His eyes widen. His mouth opens. And it doesn't hurt a bit because it's not like he's hurt. He's just shocked. I can do shock.

And then I remember that he's going to look like an idiot for telling people about my zits and that might make him squirm. I feel queasy. I turn away and take a few deep breaths. I sit down in my seat, and Mandy plops down beside me.

"What do you think, Lizzie?" she asks.

She's wearing a pink straw hat, a sweet little number with a curled brim. "Oh, cute!" I say.

"Thanks!" she says. "I got it at the mall like you said."

Note to self: Do not make the mistake of casting an honesty spell. Things are complicated enough already.

A love spell though...I gaze at Kyle and wonder. But if I did that, and he fell in love with me, I couldn't take revenge and ditch him. I must think about that. Whew. My brain sure is getting a work-out lately.

"Should we do the lab, Lizzie?" Mandy asks.

Man. *More* brain stuff. "I guess. What do we have to do?"

It turns out to be quite easy. We have to put little bits of metal on the table and pick them up with a magnet. Mr. Sparks comes by and says, "I'm impressed. You girls are working two days in a row? So, what does this experiment tell you?"

"Like attracts like?" I say.

"No," he says, "there are positive and negative forces. Only opposites attract."

"Oh," I say.

"You keep working on it," he says.
And off he goes.

I shake my head. "I think he missed
the point."

"What do you mean?" Mandy asks.

In reply, I pull a plastic tube of lip gloss
out of my purse and place it next to the
magnet. Nothing happens. "See? It's only
metal that's attracted to metal." I don't
tell her that I just figured out the main
difference between science and magick.
It's all in how you look at things.

Okay, not everything. No matter
how I look at it, Mr. Snead in room 101
is still a grump. He won't let me light
the incense.

"Smelly stuff," he says. "Likely to set
off the smoke alarms. Be seated and
remain silent."

I slump into a seat. I feel deeply sorry
for myself. I look around, and the drooling
dude is watching me. He's not drooling
anymore; instead he's giving me the eye.
I reward him with a tiny smile and when
he smiles back, omigod! He's gorgeous.

His whole face lights up. *This* must be the light Stella was talking about.

With great stealth, he rises to a crouching position and sort of duck-walks sideways. Toward me. His waddle would look really stupid if it didn't make perfect sense. Should Mr. Snead happen to glance up, the dude could freeze and it would appear that he was still seated.

He makes it to my table, and I notice that he looks quite mature. Maybe he's in grade nine? Then he smiles again, and it's breathtaking. His dark eyes crinkle at the corners, his teeth gleam white and there's this whole happy effect. It's as if he's happy on the inside and it shows on his face.

He grabs a piece of paper and scribbles a note. It says: *Hi! I'm Brendan.*

I write: *Hi, Brendan. I'm Lizzie.*

He writes back: *I've never seen you before. Where did you come from?*

He's never seen me? He must have slept through yesterday's zit disaster. Wow. He is such a *sweetie*! I'm trying to think of something cute and witty to write back when in walk Rachel and Mr. Sparks.

"Lizzie Lane?" Mr. Sparks says. "Please come with me." He mutters something to Mr. Snead and that's it. I have to leave. I cast one last glance at Brendan, and he gives me a sad wave.

Mr. Sparks takes us as far as the hall and says, "Rachel has confessed to me that she gave you the answer key. Both of us owe you an apology, Lizzie. I'm very sorry I didn't believe you." He looks at Rachel.

Rachel looks miserable. I hold up my hand. "She already apologized. Please don't make her do it again. And please don't punish her. I think she's suffered enough already."

Mr. Sparks shakes his head. "You girls are well on your way to becoming young women." Then he sighs and mutters, "Which is probably why I don't understand what just happened here. You may go."

"Um, do I have to?" I ask. "Can't I go back in room 101?"

Mr. Sparks' brow creases with worry. "Lizzie, the past couple of days must have been very hard on you. I'm going to say no to that. I think it would be best if you went home to rest. And don't worry, we'll contact your parents again, and you'll get another chance to write the exam. Off you go now."

It seems I have no choice. Rachel and I trudge away, and it turns out we don't have much to say to each other. I think we need some distance after the complete weirdness of everything. The only person I really want to see is Stella.

On the way to Stella's house, I try to decide if it's possible to forget that Brendan drooled. I mean, he's really cute, but now that we're apart, I find myself picturing that detail. Not pretty. No, it could never work between us. Mr. Sparks was right. The past couple of days have been hard on me. All of my standards are messed up.

I get to Stella's and knock on the door. The baba answers. "Ah, Lizzie. Come in. Stella is in the kitchen with Angela."

Sure enough, they're having tea and cake at the table and ask me to join them.

It's fine, right up until Angela says, "I see through your clothes."

"Why," I ask, "does she say that?"

Stella says, "It's her mantra. Baba taught her to say it. Only she's supposed to say cloak, not clothes."

"Oh," I say. Talk about lame.

"Do you know why I taught her?" the baba asks. "I'll tell you. It's a reminder to me that no matter what is seen on the surface, I must also be aware of the unseen."

"You mean, like, ghosts?" I ask.

She shrugs. "More like spirits. The higher self. The true self."

"Right," I say. "I've been thinking about that. Sort of. I'm thinking I'd like you to undo my revenge spell."

The baba looks at Stella, then back at me. "Do you really wish for this?"

"I don't like feeling the pain of others," I say. "It upsets me."

"None of us like it," Stella says.

"It is almost impossible to undo a revenge spell," says the baba. "I may make things worse for you. The question you must consider is, does it serve the higher purpose?"

"I'll get back to you on that." I fiddle with my tea cup and say, "But that's enough about *me*. What I want to know is how did Stella know about *me*? That I had this hidden talent?"

Stella smiles. "Like I said, my gift is finding the gift in others. Even though you'd only used the talent to predict trends, I sensed the power in you." She looks sideways at her baba then asks, "So, Lizzie, do you know anyone who suffers from being self-centered?"

I roll my eyes. "Practically everyone I know has that problem."

"Really?" She shakes her head. "Do you think that might *hurt* them?"

I consider this. "Yes. Yes, I think it would hurt them. I mean, it might make it hard for them to have friends. And I'll bet it's super hard for them to get a boyfriend."

"So," Stella says, "when you think about how these people have such a hard time, does it hurt *you*?"

I stare at her. I think about it. A little tear forms in my eye and I sniffle. "It must be awful for them."

Stella and her baba nod.

"I know what we could do," I say. "I mean, before this whole empathy thing *kills* me. We could cast a spell to, you know, fix them. Then they wouldn't bother me anymore."

Stella grins and leans forward. "Great idea, Lizzie. I know the perfect spell."

"Cool," I say. "Let's do it."

Acknowledgments:

My gratitude also to Kendra Anderson for reading an early draft and to Melanie Jeffs, Orca Editor, for working her fine magick.

K.L. Denman has written numerous books for kids, including *Mirror Image*, *Rebel's Tag* and *The Shade* in the Orca Currents series. She lives in Powell River, British Columbia.

Orca Currents

121 Express
Monique Polak

Bio-pirate
Michele Martin Bossley

Camp Wild
Pam Withers

Chat Room
Kristin Butcher

Cracked
Michele Martin Bossley

Crossbow
Dayle Campbell Gaetz

Daredevil Club
Pam Withers

Dog Walker
Karen Spafford-Fitz

Explore
Christy Goerzen

Finding Elmo
Monique Polak

Flower Power
Ann Walsh

Horse Power
Ann Walsh

Orca Currents

Hypnotized
Don Trembath

In a Flash
Eric Walters

Laggan Lard Butts
Eric Walters

Manga Touch
Jacqueline Pearce

Marked
Norah McClintock

Mirror Image
K.L. Denman

Nine Doors
Vicki Grant

Pigboy
Vicki Grant

Perfect Revenge
K.L. Denman

Queen of the Toilet Bowl
Frieda Wishinsky

Rebel's Tag
K.L. Denman

See No Evil
Diane Young

Orca Currents

Sewer Rats
Sigmund Brouwer

The Shade
K.L. Denman

Skate Freak
Lesley Choyce

Special Edward
Eric Walters

Splat!
Eric Walters

Spoiled Rotten
Dayle Campbell Gaetz

Sudden Impact
Lesley Choyce

Swiped
Michele Martin Bossley

Watch Me
Norah McClintock

Wired
Sigmund Brouwer

Visit www.orcabook.com for all Orca titles.